Desperate Measures

AMY LAURENS

OTHER WORKS

SANCTUARY SERIES

Where Shadows Rise
Through Roads Between
When Worlds Collide

KADITEOS SERIES

How Not To Acquire A Castle

STORM FOXES SERIES

A Fox of Storms and Starlight
A Stag Of Hope And Memory

SHORTER WORKS

April Showers
Darkness And Good
Dreaming Of Forests
Of Sea Foam And Blood
Trust Issues

NON-FICTION

How To Write Dogs
How To Theme
How To Create Cultures
How To Create Life
How To Map
The 32 Worst Mistakes People Make About Dogs

Find other works by the author at
www.amylaurens.com

Desperate Measures

INKLET #68

AMY LAURENS

Inkprint PRESS
www.inkprintpress.com

Print ISBN: 978-1-925825-75-6
eBook ISBN: 9798201987824

www.inkprintpress.com

National Library of Australia Cataloguing-in-Publication Data
Laurens, Amy 1985 –
Desperate Measures
56 p.
ISBN: 978-1-925825-75-6
Inkprint Press, Canberra, Australia
1. Fiction—Horror 2. Fiction—Fantasy—Dark Fantasy
3. Fiction—Short Stories

First Print Edition: October 2021
Cover photo © 明辉 李 via Pixabay
Cover design © Inkprint Press
Interior art © Amy Laurens

DESPERATE MEASURES

As always, Katrina gazed in awe at the rows of white dresses that lined the walls, some sparkling, some shimmering—all beautiful. She gripped her mother's arm and squealed. "That's it, that's my dress right there!" She pointed toward a mannequin at the back of the store.

Her mother smiled. "Come on."

The sales assistants, in their crisp black suits and white cotton gloves, were all busy with other customers, and a young blonde girl smiled apologetically. "I'm sorry ma'am, we'll be with you in a moment."

Katrina didn't mind. She adored bridal stores—could spend *hours* in them, literally. Ever since she'd been a bridesmaid for Tanya two years ago, she'd been addicted.

She leaned against the counter. Honestly, the way some of those dresses glittered—especially that puffy-skirted one on the mannequin—well, she wouldn't find it hard to believe they were alive.

A flicker caught her eye, and she looked down toward the mirrors at the back of the store. A thirty-some-thing woman with dark, glossy hair posed, primping the veil in her hair. The sales assistant stooped behind her, adjusting the train and hemline.

Katrina smiled again.

The snug fitting bodice showed off the woman's curves perfectly, and the golden ivory of the satin made her tanned skin glow.

And the crystalling down the back… Katrina sighed wistfully. Her parents weren't exactly oozing cash, and she and her fiancé lived the frugal life of students. Her dress was pretty—but it was plain.

The woman in front of the mirrors turned, flicking the train of the dress out behind her. The crystal beading caught the light, writhing like some fantastical snake around the hem and stirring envy in Katrina's breast.

"Katrina?"

She turned back to the counter. A dark-haired, stern-faced assistant arched an eyebrow and peered over her glasses.

Katrina nodded. "Yes, that's me." She swallowed, suddenly nervous.

"And you're here to pick up…" The assistant glanced down at the open book on the table. "A *Glamorique* gown and veil?"

Katrina nodded again, throat dry.

The assistant gave a curt jerk of her chin. "I presume you wish to try it on? When was the wedding, again?"

"Er, tomorrow."

The woman's eyebrows shot up in surprise.

"Yes, there, er, there were some issues."

"I see." The assistant stared.

Katrina shuffled. "Um, I'd like to try it on?"

"I'll go fetch it, then." One more glance at the book, then she disappeared into the back room.

Her mother squeezed Katrina's arm. "It'll be okay," she said. "This time it will be fine."

Katrina nodded, hoping she was right.

She *should* be right. There was no reason for her not to be.

But there had been no reason for her to be wrong *last* week, either. *Or* the week before that.

Katrina's stomach twisted, and she wished the friendly sales assistant would appear. She'd been so kind last week when Katrina had opened the zip-up bag, only to find they'd sent the wrong dress.

And she'd been wonderful the week *before* that when the gown had been the right style, but so tiny Katrina couldn't even get it over her shoulders.

The sales assistant emerged from the back room, arms overflowing with a white plastic zip-up bag. She strode off towards the change rooms.

"Off you go," said Mum in a low voice. "Here, I'll take your bag."

Katrina passed over her handbag and sunglasses, and took a long, deep breath. "I hope it's okay this time."

"It will be," said Mum. "It'll be fine."

Katrina squared her shoulders, and marched after the assistant.

As she entered the change room, a movement caught her eye. She looked at the mirrors that covered the back wall. They showed nothing out of the ordinary—just a perfect reflection of the empty store.

That was odd… Katrina creased her brow. When had that dark haired woman left?

But the sales assistant had lifted the dress up and stared at her impatiently. Katrina jerked the curtain shut, shrugged out of her cotton day-dress and held up her arms.

You'd think after so many fittings I'd have ceased to feel vulnerable, she thought, standing with her arms above her head in nothing but a strapless bra and knickers. *Apparently not.* She shivered, even though the store was warm, and was glad when the satin dropped over her shoulders.

Over her shoulders, over her hips… It kept dropping, dropping, until at last it stopped, gathering around her upper thighs.

Katrina looked down at the dress, then up at the sales assistant, stomach sinking.

"Um, that's not supposed to happen, is it?" The dress was supposed to be figure hugging. And in order for it to hug her waist, there was no *way* it ought to be able to fall down over her hips like that.

The sales assistant pursed her lips and took hold of the back of the dress. "Let's do it up first," she said.

She lifted the dress up so it covered Katrina's torso, and Katrina hugged it to hold it up. She heard the zipper screaming up its track—but the dress didn't seem to be getting any tighter.

"Hmm."

Katrina's pulse quickened. "What?"

The assistant's fingers scrabbled at the inside of the dress. "What size did you say you ordered?"

"Twelve," Katrina said, lifting her arms up, holding them away from the dress to keep the sweat off the precious satin. "Why?"

"Hmm."

"*What?*"

"The label says sixteen. I'm terribly sorry."

Katrina took a deep breath. *I am* not *going to cry. I'm not.* She glanced up at her reflection in the tiny plate-sized mirror that hung in the change room. *Not going to smash mirrors, either.* She exhaled. "Ok. What can I do?"

"You said the wedding is tomorrow?"

She nodded.

"Then I'm afraid there's not much we *can* do. If you'd come earlier in the day"—Katrina felt like smacking her for that accusatory tone—"then we could have had a seamstress work at it all day to take it in. But now…" She shrugged.

Katrina clenched her jaw, fighting tears and the urge to tear the stupid dress right down the seams.

"Although…" The sales woman tilted her head.

Katrina's heart leaped at the speculative tone. "What, what is it?"

She hesitated, chewing on her lip.

Katrina blinked in surprise. The women who worked in bridal stores were always so professional, so snooty, so *perfect*. Chewing lower lips seemed right out of character—and it worried her.

"Katrina? How's it going?"

Her mother's concerned voice reeled her back to earth with a crash. The wedding was *tomorrow*. She didn't care what the sales assistant was feeling; if she could help somehow, anyhow, she was willing to hear it. "Um, can't quite tell yet, Mum. I'll be out in a minute!" Katrina turned to the sales woman. "Can you do anything or not?" She placed a hand on her hip and tried to project assertiveness.

"I... Well, yes," said the assistant. "But it's not exactly something we would recommend to anyone, and, in fact, we usually don't like to think about it at all, but since your situation is so desperate, maybe it's worth a try."

Katrina frowned. Babbling was even *less* consistent with her mental image of bridal shop assistants. What on earth was going on? Katrina exhaled forcefully. "Look, if it's going to make this dress miraculously fit me between now and one o'clock tomorrow after-noon, I'm willing to try it. Whatever 'it' is."

The woman's face tightened and she gave a curt nod. "We'll go out then. But it might... take a while. You..."

She swallowed, and Katrina's stomach clenched. "You'd probably better ask your mother to leave. They don't like… extras."

Extras? Now Katrina was beyond confused. "You want me to tell my mother, who has practically organised this wedding single-handedly, who hasn't slept in the last three days, who is just as stressed about this dress as I am, to go away?" She raised an eyebrow.

The sales woman nodded. "Please trust me. It's much safer that way."

Safer? This was starting to sound crazy.

Maybe it was. Maybe she should just duck down to the formal wear shop tomorrow morning and purchase the first dress that was white and fitted. Maybe—

"Katrina? Are you quite sure everything's fine?"

She took a deep breath. "Uh, Mum?"

Footsteps, and then the curtain wavered. "Yes, dear?" she said from right outside.

"Well, it's not a *big* deal, it's just minor, they just need to do a slight re-fit. But it's going to take a while."

"But we need to pick the flowers up before five!"

"I know. You go on. I'll stay here with the dress. It'll be fine."

"Okay. Message me when you're done and I'll come pick you up, okay?"

"Sure Mum, thanks."

"Here's your bag."

Katrina took it and dropped it in a corner of the change room. "Thanks. Bye."

"Bye."

She waited until she heard the bell that hung over the front door of the shop ring, then turned to the sales assistant. "Well? I hope whatever you have in mind is worth it."

The assistant nodded and smiled. "Definitely."

Katrina felt she'd have believed the woman if her face hadn't been so pale.

The woman swiped back the curtain. "Go hop up on the step."

Katrina gathered up the skirt in her fingertips and tiptoed towards the raised step that took pride of place in front of the mirrors.

The carpet felt scratchy and comfortting under her feet, and she rubbed her toes against the edge of the step before stepping onto it. She released the skirt and it draped to the floor, the hem brushing the carpet. Behind, the assistant fussed over the train, straightening and tidying and brushing of stray bits of fluff.

Why bother? thought Katrina, struck by melancholy now that she could see her reflection. She held her arms out.

The dress dropped, revealing a good two inches of bra. *She's never going to be able to take this in enough overnight.*

The assistant took her time fussing, and Katrina grew distracted. The sky outside had dimmed—probably a storm, and she hoped fervently once again that the weather would stay fine tomorrow—and the lights around the mirrors seemed to yellow.

The dresses on the racks and mannequins glittered and sparkled and for a moment Katrina was sure that they moved... Surely they couldn't sparkle like that by themselves.

With half closed eyes, Katrina looked back at her reflection and tilted her head.

Hm. The dress didn't look so bad.

She smiled dreamily at the shimmering satin. Okay, so it didn't have crystal beading, and it was devoid of lace or sequins or decoration of any sort...

But it was beautiful in its simplicity.

The woman came up beside Katrina, a strange look on her face. "Keep quiet," she said. "They're coming."

The tight, haunted look in her eyes spoke to Katrina's subconscious and she responded with her voice low and urgent. "What's happening?"

"They're coming," the woman said again.

"Who?"

The sky outside darkened and thunder rumbled. The building trembled, the motion setting the dresses on the racks dancing. The sparkles and glitterings went wild with the movement, and the mirror bloomed with white and gold fireworks.

Katrina blinked, trying to clear the blinding lights from her eyes.

"They're here."

The woman's voice was hoarse, and Katrina turned. She strained, trying to see the woman past the afterimages burned in her vision. Through the flashes she thought she saw fear, raw and open, on the woman's face.

The spots faded, and Katrina looked more closely—but the woman's face seemed calm now—if it had even been different before.

"*Who* are here?" Katrina demanded.

The woman's eyes gleamed. She smiled, slow and dangerous. "We are."

Adrenalin shot through Katrina's body. The woman's voice was no longer a tense soprano. Instead, it was rich and deep—and had a strange, echoing quality.

Katrina swallowed. "Um, we?"

"Yes."

The echoes behind the voice sent shivers up and down Katrina's spine, and she turned back to the mirror to avoid the woman's intense gaze.

The woman shifted, and in the mirror it looked for a moment like she had numerous limbs, like there was more than a single person occupying her space. "What is it you want?"

Before Katrina could answer, thunder cracked again.

The dresses on the racks shuddered and in the mirror—Katrina gulped—the beading that snaked around the hem of the dress on the nearest mannequin was *actually snaking*.

"I will ask you again." The woman stepped up nose-to-nose with Katrina. "What is it that you desire?"

"I... I..." Surely her *eyes* couldn't be shimmering?

"Oh come now," said the woman. "You must want *some*thing. Beads, perhaps?" She touched a finger to the side seam of the gown, beads sprouting and spreading down Katrina's hip.

Katrina gasped.

"No?" The woman arched an eyebrow. "Crystals?" she said, drawing her fingers over the neckline of the strapless dress. A few tiny crystals sprang into being, and she tilted her head. "More, maybe?"

Katrina's heart hammered and she jerked away. The woman pressed harder and despite her fear, Katrina's body rippled in response. Within moments, the fabric was encrusted in crystals.

Katrina moaned softly.

The woman glanced up, lips quirking at the corners. "No?" she said. "Then what?"

Katrina panted, chest heaving, legs tingling. "I... I just... I just want it to fit."

"Want what to fit?" she said.

"The... the dress. I want it tighter." Her heart hammered harder 'til she thought it might break through her breastbone.

The woman pressed her fingertips down and Katrina moaned again. "I can do tighter." She placed her hands around Katrina's waist and the fabric of the dress writhed under her palms, shrinking and tightening.

The satin caressed Katrina's skin and she shuddered. Even through the fear, it felt *good*.

She drew in a breath, trying to calm herself. As she exhaled, the bodice closed around her ribs, her breasts, her waist and hips...

She tried to breathe in again. "Tight."

The woman laughed and held her tighter. "Oh, you are a precious one."

"No," she gasped. "*Too* tight."

She flinched as the woman reached up to brush her cheek. "*Never* too tight, my pretty one."

The dresses in the mirror danced to the thunder, shimmering, flashing, glittering. The woman stooped and ran a finger around the hem of the gown, beads slithering out behind her fingers. They spread, unfurling like a vine, climbing, creeping, trailing, up and up towards Katrina's hips, around her waist, over the rise of her breasts, and onwards.

Katrina squeaked, batting them down. But the beads, free of the dress, continued their upwards climb, twining themselves through her hair, wrapping around her neck. She screamed. "Stop! Stop, make it stop!"

The woman laughed. "Oh, I will my dear. When your dress is quite tight enough." She placed her hands around Katrina's waist again.

"It *is,*" Katrina choked out, tears streaming down her cheeks. "It is! Please, please stop!"

The woman leaned over Katrina's shoulder and caught her eye in the mirror. "*Never* too tight, remember? You asked for tight. Tight it is."

"I'm sorry!" Katrina cried, slapping at the beads that now crawled up her face, over her nose and into her ears. "I'm sorry, just make it stop!"

The woman laughed, a deep velvety sound. "That, my dear, is what you get for approaching the spirit of the bridal store." She stepped back and clapped her hands.

The beads crawled faster, reaching up Katrina's nose.

She opened her mouth to scream, but the beads drowned her out. She sucked in a last gasp of air, clawing frantically at her throat as she inhaled the beads, choking, coughing, falling to the floor as they suffocated her...

And the woman stood over her, and laughed.

THE MAKING OF *DESPERATE MEASURES*

This story, to be honest, is cursed, and I half expect that in the publishing of it, something horrible is going to happen to Inkprint Press that will take it under. Or perhaps this is a case of "third time's the charm".

Because, you see, this story sold not once, but twice, back in the early days of my fiction career, and *both* times, within about a month of accepting this story, the publication that had done so closed. And so it never did get published, at least not until now (I hope. Fingers crossed. Etc.).

The *setting* of this story is very closely based on my experiences accompanying my sister-in-law on a shopping expedition for her wedding dress. The *events*, however, are far removed, because that experience was actually entirely delightful, and utterly devoid of anything negative at all—particularly vengeful bridal store horrors.

I still feel sorry for poor Katrina. All she wanted was a pretty dress.

Read more by Amy Laurens!

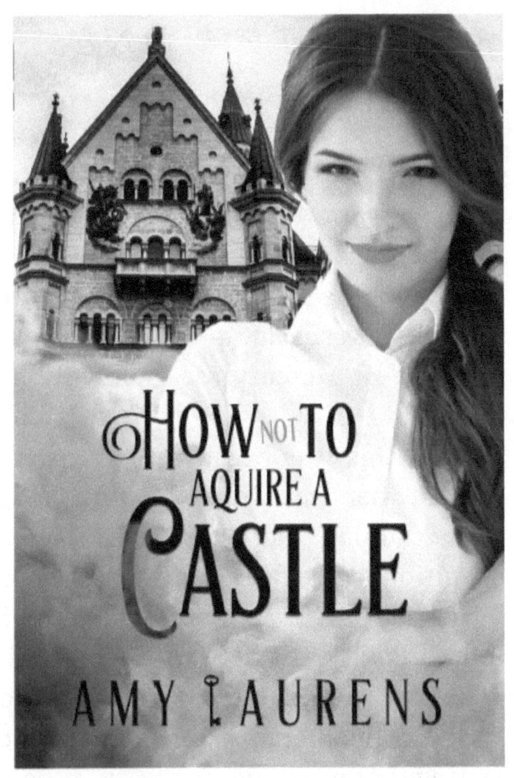

HOW NOT TO ACQUIRE A CASTLE

CHAPTER ONE

ON A HARD PLASTIC CHAIR IN THE FRONT row of the Great Hall in the world's fifth-best evil overlording academy, with its red-wooden parquetry floor that spoke of wealth and the beige, square panels of sound-boards speaking of conservatism on the walls, Mercury sat, pointedly not sweating.

Partly, this was because the Academy Administrators had deigned to turn on the air-conditioning earlier in the day, in recognition of the fact that the hall would be packed out with approximately six hundred bodies, all here to celebrate the graduation of about a third of that crowd.

But mostly, Mercury was pointedly not sweating because she made it a point never to sweat, sweat being an indication that she was working hard, and hard work being antithetical to her way of life.

However. If she *had* been sweating right now, it would not have been due to the uncomfortable warmth of six hundred packed bodies that even the air-conditioning system couldn't completely shift, or, in fact, from overexertion. Instead, it would have been caused by an even more unfamiliar concept in Mercury's emotional vocabulary: nervousness.

Mercury did not *get* nervous. Mercury got things *done*.

So the fact that she was sitting here, in the front row of the Great Hall, about to graduate from Evil Overlording Academy (with distinction), and was feeling *nervous*... She crumpled the black paper program in her pale fists. It made her furious, that's what it did.

Abjectly furious, that snooty-tooty Deviran with his stupid morals and his stupid I-don't-want-to-be-here and his stupid Overlords-are-empty-figureheads and his stupid face sitting ten people over, looking implacable with his deep brown skin and barely-there, precision-groomed beard, as though he knew it gave him a stupid air of alluringly stupid mystery...

Mercury scowled and searched for the train of thought that had been derailed, yet again, by Deviran's stupidity.

Ah. Yes. She was angry because she was nervous because she wasn't absolutely entirely one hundred and fifty percent sure that she'd beaten Deviran in their final exams, and 1) being anything less than a hundred and fifty percent certain of anything made her cranky, and 2) being beaten by Deviran for dux of the year would be utterly unbearable. She flicked away a piece of fluff that had become snagged under her immaculately magenta-painted nails and smoothed out the black paper program.

In the front corner of the hall, the starkly-attired string quartet with their traditional black instruments began playing the March of the Oncoming Doom. The screechy scrapes of hundreds of chairs on the hall's wooden floor sounded as the crowd climbed to its collective feet.

Mercury sat with her arms firmly folded for a few moments longer, until her best friend Sparky kicked her in the ankle.

"Get up, idiot," Sparky hissed, hints of real flame flickering through her flame-coloured pixie cut.

"No," Mercury said, flouncing to her feet and tossing her own glossy brown hair back over her shoulders. Four years she'd been playing by the Academy's rules in order to get what she wanted, and she'd had just about enough. Other people's rules should only be applied to plebs too stupid to invent their own.

Sparky rolled her eyes somewhere over Mercury's head before focusing on the stage, where the ceremonial party had begun entering.

Mercury clenched her jaw and narrowed her own eyes as the teachers of the Evil Overlording Academy filed onto the stage, dressed in their formal finery. Each teacher had their own distinctive look that matched their personality and their Overlording style, from severe charcoal suits to jet-black leathers, pastel ball-gowns and gem-toned lingerie and eye-blinding spandex, and even on one tiny old woman at the back, worn jeans and a grey flannel shirt. She was the one to watch out for, of course; Mercury could respect an Overlord who was confident enough in their abilities that they didn't need to telegraph them. It wasn't a look *she* would consider, of course, but still. She could respect it.

The band's march finished and, after a moderately awkward pause, the crowd sat. The Principal, pale skin and dark hair matching his suspiciously vampiric red-and-black suit, took the podium, and Mercury narrowed her eyes. He was doing a superb job of hiding his emotions—he was a premier Evil Overlord, after all—but she was Mercury, and unlike anyone else, she had the benefit of being able to rummage through people's conscious-nesses. She was better at adding things *into* people's minds than taking infor-mation out, but he was telegraphing fear loudly enough that she could sense it without trying overly much.

Mercury pursed her lips.
Hmm.

The Principal cleared his throat at the blackened-wood podium, and the fear made it into his usually-unreadable eyes. "Before we begin," he said, and Mercury's stomach did a peculiar kind of flip-flop. "I have a pressing announcement to make regarding the safety of our students and their families."

He cleared his throat again and took out a sheet of paper from his pocket, unfolding it carefully and smoothing out the creases before beginning again. "The Council"—quiet booing echoed around the hall, and Mercury tsked impatiently— "have asked me to recommend that students from Tumul Tuos seriously consider postponing their return to town for a few days. The city is dealing with a *situation* at present which may present a danger to our students' health and safety."

Mercury's hands fisted at her sides and she forced herself to remain seated. What was wrong with her city? What had the Council mucked up now? A risk to the students' safety? There had to be more he wasn't telling them. Gently, Mercury tugged on his consciousness, implanting the suggestion that it might be better to share the news than to keep it secret. After all, how could they fight an enemy they didn't know?

"There are, ah..." He trailed off, glancing side to side as though wondering why his mouth had decided to continue.

Mercury didn't snicker, but she did press her lips together in satisfaction.

The Principal took a deep, steadying breath and seemed to change tack. "There has been one death already. The family have already been notified, so it is with much regret that I must inform you that Woovermyer will no longer be with us at the Evil Overlording Academy."

Murmurs broke out around the room, not all of them sad—to be expected in a school devoted to raising the next generation of dictators (ish) and despots (of sorts).

Mercury, however, crushed her program in her left hand, fist so tight her nails bit her palm.

"You okay?" Sparky murmured.

Mercury gave a single, tense shake of her head and stared at the podium. Dead. Livie Woovermyer was dead in *her city*. And the Council hadn't done anything to stop it. Couldn't do anything to stop it, probably, given they'd warned the students to stay away. Livie hadn't been the strongest candidate in the year level, but she was no lightweight, either. It would take a lot of power to kill a Seven.

Enough was enough. A good thing Mercury was about to graduate at the top of the class, giving her the right to knock the lowest ranking current Overlord off their perch. Tumul Tuos would be hers in a matter of hours. And then there'd be no more of these wasteful deaths. Her city would be safe at last.

Madame Pompadour was up the front now, elbow gloves the same glimmery silver colour as her elaborate, piled-curls wig, eyelids gleaming with matching silver eye shadow, and abruptly Mercury realised Madame was there to make the announcement that would change her life forever. She leaned forward in her seat, ready to stand when her name was called.

"And now the announcement you've all been dying for," the Political Alliances teacher trilled, the frills on her evening gown fluttering as she moved. "The dux of this year's cohort!"

Sweat slicked Mercury's palms. Irritated, she reached over and wiped them on Sparky's thigh.

Sparky pushed Mercury's hands back into her own personal space bubble and Mercury, nervous to the edge of distraction, let her.

"Will you please join me in welcoming to the stage, our wonderful dux for this year, Deviran Goodsmith!"

Mercury froze halfway to standing. "Did she just say Deviran?" she whispered furiously to Sparky.

Sparky hauled her forcibly back down into her seat. "Yes," she hissed back. "Sit down, you're making a fool of yourself."

Mercury's spine snapped upright as she sat, and she arranged the folds of her long black skirt demurely. "No I'm not." She closed her eyes. "Deviran's going up to the stage, isn't he?" Even at a whisper, the misery in her voice was clear, but this time, she didn't care.

Sparky reached over and squeezed her hand.

Mercury squeezed back, lacing her fingers through Sparky's, and held tight as all her plans and dreams vanished in front of her.

A stone had landed in her chest. That must be it. Some strange sort of magic that made her chest contract and sink, and made the world distort for just a moment, long enough to trick her into thinking Deviran had beaten her so that someone could jump in front of her and yell SURPRISE!

Any moment now.

Any moment.

She refused to open her eyes and watch Deviran parading across the stupid stage like some stupid stupid-person, receiving his stupid medal and stupid symbolic crest pin.

It was that last exam question.

She'd known Deviran would pull out his ridiculous 'Evil Overlords are merely figureheads, the Business Guild is where the power really lies' rant that everyone had heard a million times back when he was younger and angrier, and she'd tried to counter it, she really had.

She'd argued for the importance of the Overlording position, for the power of having a symbolic figure to unite the population in their hatred, for having a person able to make all the difficult, necessary decisions the Council was too weak and spineless to make... But it hadn't been enough. Everything she'd worked for, everything she'd set out to prove—and it wasn't enough.

There were words, there were names, and then forever later, once she'd died twice already, Sparky elbowed her in the ribs. "Come on," Sparky muttered. "We're up next."

And sure enough, there was a shuffling of presenters as the last of the Powers Behind The Thone graduates departed the stage, and the next speaker announced in

threatening, funereal tones, "The Overlording cohort."

Mercury blinked furiously and followed
Sparky to the end of the line at the right
side of the stage. The other candidates
proceeded one at a time across the stage,
two girls and then stupid Deviran, and
then a handful more and then Sparky, and
then the speaker was calling her name.

Hands fisted, Mercury tossed her head
high, climbed the four steps, and marched
across the stage. She wouldn't look at
them, the stupid faculty who'd denied her
the city she rightfully deserved, and she
wouldn't look the other way either, at the
classmates and crowd undoubtedly snig-
gering at her failure.

She shook hands with the presenter,
and while he pinned the tiny crossed-
swords badge on her collar, her eyes
betrayed her and slid towards the aud-
ience. Her stomach flipped as she saw the
crowd of parents and friends behind the
rows of students, all the way to the back
of the hall, twenty rows at least, illum-
inated by the late afternoon light stream-

ing in through the ceiling-high windows to the right. Everyone had someone here to watch them graduate. Everyone except Weird Al—and her.

The presenter finished with her pin, muttered something to her, and offered his hand again. Mercury coldly ignored it and strode from the stage. It didn't matter. None of it mattered. Tumul Tuos was her city anyway, and no one could change that. She'd think of something. She'd take a day or two out, make some plans...

And she could always hope that Deviran would choose some other Overlording territory. He'd be stupid to, but then again, he was stupid, so. Mercury could hope.

All at once, mid-way down the steps off the stage, Mercury came to rigid attention, scanning the room. Somewhere out there in the crowd, an exchange of power had just taken place, and it felt... unusual.

But the final few students were backing up behind her and muttering, so Mercury headed back toward her seat, craning her head all the while and searching for some sign of whatever it was that had just discharged a dizzyingly quiet amount of power into the room.

She sat, and Sparky leaned over. "Okay?"

"Mm," said Mercury. "Did you feel…" She accidentally caught the eye of the student behind her and twisted back to face the front.

"Feel what?"

Mercury turned it over in her mind. It had felt like a large shot of power discharged very quietly—but perhaps it hadn't been. Perhaps it had only been a small discharge after all, something most people wouldn't have noticed.

But still, something about it had tugged on her. It very nearly felt like something she'd felt before, only she *knew* she'd never sensed that kind of discharge before.

She shook her head. "Never mind. Don't worry."

Sparky sighed and straightened. "It's fine, Mercury," she said, drily exasperated.

"I know you didn't win, but I promise, you'll live through it."

Mercury waved a hand for silence.

The power had just discharged again, and it had come from somewhere in the back corner, far away from the windows and light.

Impatiently, Mercury waited for the formalities to conclude. The crowd stood while the quartet played the exit march, and the stage party left, Mercury tapping her foot all the while.

The moment the last notes of the march died away, Mercury turned and headed to the back corner, weaving in and out of the students and parents who had seemed to explode slowly but inexorably out from the neat rows of seating, ignoring Sparky's calls behind her. Power, something that tugged in a way that was strange and familiar, all at once. She pushed her way through a family posing for pictures—and halted.

In the shadows of the back corner, Deviran stood with his family, with his stupid, smug little smile, looking as tall and dark and stupidly alluring as ever. Prat.

His mother, short but sleek, and his father—tall, and utterly terrifying in a way not at all diminished by his gleaming smile—gushed over him, patting his back and hugging him tight. Within moments the Principal was there, glibly shaking hands and congratulating them on the success of their son. Something flickered across his consciousness, and also Deviran's father's—some moment of recognition in response to what they were saying.

But Mercury brushed it aside just as the mother brushed melodramatic tears from her cheeks and handed Deviran a silver-wrapped package about as long as her hand but half the width.

That. That was the source of the strange, magical feeling. Mercury watched hawk-eyed as Deviran un-wrapped the gift. A glimpse of gold set her pulse racing—What was it? What did it do? Could she steal it?—and then the paper fell away to the floor, and Deviran stood staring wordlessly at the object in his hands, and Mercury did too.

Wide-eyed, Deviran raised his gaze to his parents, and even from where she stood Mercury could hear the reverence in his voice as he thanked them.

But Mercury had eyes only for the object. No wonder she'd felt it discharge, and no wonder it had felt both strange and familiar. In Deviran's hands lay a glorious, sunshine-gold key, large and strong—and with a handle in the shape of a stylised fish, long, flowing fins curving to make the grip.

A Key. They'd given him a Key. And not just any Key, but *the* Key, *her* Key, the Artefact of Power belonging to *her* city.

A wordless noise of wanting rose in Mercury's throat. Who cared about being dux? She needed that Key.

Keep reading! Head to
www.amylaurens.com/books/kaditeos/castle
to buy your copy now!

ABOUT THE AUTHOR

AMY LAURENS is an Australian author of fantasy fiction for all ages. She doesn't usually write horror, but very occasionally something dark like this bubbles up from heretoforth unexplored corners of her mind and the most practical way to dispense of it is to write it down.

Amy has also written the award-winning portal-fantasy *Sanctuary* series about Edge, a 13-year-old girl forced to move to a country town because of witness protection (the first book is *Where Shadows Rise*); the humorous fantasy *Kaditeos* series, following newly graduated Evil Overlord Mercury as she attempts to acquire a castle; the young adult series *Storm Foxes*, about love and magic and family in small town Australia, and a host of non-fiction.

INKLETS

Collect them all! Released on the 1st and 15th of each month.

INKLET #055
Allure
AMY LAURENS

INKLET #056
The LIES We KNOW
LIANA BROOKS

DOUBLE ISSUE
INKLET #057
AFTERMATH & Fool Me Once
AMY LAURENS

INKLET #058
Purity
An Age Of Unicorns Story
AMY LAURENS

INKLET #059
Saved
AMY LAURENS

INKLET #060
A Kiss is the Secret
AMY LAURENS

INKLET #061
A Changing Tides Story
Fire Bright
AMY LAURENS

INKLET #062
Hades AND Persephone
LIANA BROOKS

INKLET #063
Just So Long As You're Happy
AMY LAURENS

INKLET #064
Theft Of A Lifetime
LIANA BROOKS

INKLET #065
Shoe
AMY LAURENS

INKLET #066
Published AUTHOR
LIANA BROOKS

DOUBLE INKLET
INKLET #067
THE REMARKABLE INSIGHT OF JELLYBEANS & Understanding
AMY LAURENS

INKLET #068
Desperate Measures
AMY LAURENS

INKLET #069
Rock-a-bye
LIANA BROOKS

INKLET #070
the Other Carly
AMY LAURENS

INKLET #071
B's By Bioluminescent Light
AMY LAURENS

INKLET #072
Even Villains Grant Wishes
A Heroes & Villains Story
LIANA BROOKS